A Proper Princess

First published in 2010
by Wayland

Text copyright © Karen Wallace
Illustration copyright © Cathy Brett

Wayland
338 Euston Road
London NW1 3BH

Wayland Australia
Level 17/207 Kent Street
Sydney, NSW 2000

Series Editor: Louise John
Editor: Katie Powell
Cover design: Paul Cherrill
Design: D.R.ink
Consultant: Shirley Bickler

A CIP catalogue record for this book is available from the British Library.

ISBN 9780750263214

Printed in China

Wayland is a division of Hachette Children's Books,
an Hachette UK Company

www.hachette.co.uk

A Proper Princess

Written by Karen Wallace
Illustrated by Cathy Brett

WAYLAND

Characters

 Princess PJ: A tomboy princess

 Prince Dandyfop: A weedy prince

 King Crusty: A forgetful king

 Queen Clementine: A stuffy queen

 Princess Tiara: A visiting princess

 Storyteller

 Storyteller: Princess PJ lives in a castle. One morning, at breakfast, Queen Clementine tells everyone Princess Tiara is coming to stay. Princess PJ isn't very pleased!

Princess PJ: I bet Princess Tiara will be a **girly** princess. What will we do together? She'll hate hunting dragons and horse riding. I won't like her at all.

 Queen Clementine: Nonsense, PJ! Her mother is my best friend. Be nice to Princess Tiara, and you'll get along famously!

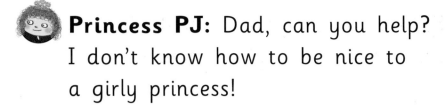 **Princess PJ:** Dad, can you help? I don't know how to be nice to a girly princess!

King Crusty: Well, let's see. You could...

Storyteller: But King Crusty forgot what he was about to say!

Prince Dandyfop: Why don't **you** pretend to be a girly princess?

 Princess PJ: You know what, Dandyfop? That's not a bad idea!

 Storyteller: Later that day there was a knock on the castle door.

 Queen Clementine: Welcome, Princess Tiara.

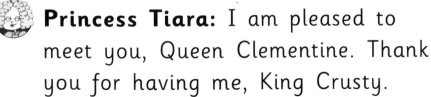 **Princess Tiara:** I am pleased to meet you, Queen Clementine. Thank you for having me, King Crusty.

 **King Crusty:** My pleasure, Princess um...

11

Storyteller: At that moment, Princess PJ walked into the room.

 Princess PJ: Hello. I'm PJ.

 Storyteller: Queen Clementine couldn't believe her eyes. PJ was wearing a dress and curtseying! The queen was so shocked, she toppled off her throne.

King Crusty: Quick, Dandyfop. You get the queen's arms and I'll um...

 Prince Dandyfop: ...get her feet?

 Storyteller: With a big-heave ho, they lifted the queen to her feet.

Storyteller: Princess PJ felt a bit strange in her frilly dress. At first she couldn't think of anything to say.

 Princess PJ: Um, what would you like to do today?

 Princess Tiara: I don't mind. Whatever you like.

 Prince Dandyfop: Let's play with my dolls' house!

Storyteller: Princess PJ, Princess Tiara and Prince Dandyfop are in the nursery. PJ and Tiara are bored as they watch Dandyfop play with his dolls' house. Just then, Queen Clementine walks in.

Queen Clementine: Girls, I'm having a party tonight. You can dress up and dance with lots of princes.

 Princes Dandyfop: I love parties! I think I'll get dressed up, too!

Princess PJ: I've had enough of talking about parties! I'm sorry, Dandyfop, but I can't stay here any longer. Playing with your dolls' house is so boring.

Storyteller: Princess PJ stood up and, to her amazement, so did Princess Tiara.

 Princess Tiara: Wherever you're going, I'm going! I hate dolls' houses, too!

Storyteller: Princess PJ and Princess Tiara ran out into the castle grounds. It was raining and they were soon soaking wet, but Princess Tiara didn't seem to mind.

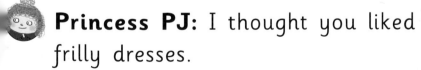 **Princess PJ:** I thought you liked frilly dresses.

Princess Tiara: No way! I'm only wearing this one because my mother made me.

Storyteller: Suddenly Princess PJ had a brilliant idea!

 Princess PJ: What do you think of muddy puddles?

 Princess Tiara: Muddy puddles? I love them!

Storyteller: So Princess PJ and Princess Tiara splashed about in the puddles, kicking muddy water at each other.

Princess PJ: Oh, bother, my dress is ruined. Mum's going to be cross!

 Princess Tiara: Never mind our dresses! We'd better run or we'll be late for the party!

Storyteller: And, just like that, PJ and Tiara became the best of friends. They raced back to the castle hand in hand.

Storyteller: In the castle, the ballroom was filled with people from all over the land.

 Queen Clementine: Just you wait until you see Princess PJ and Princess Tiara. They are the prettiest princesses in the kingdom.

Prince Dandyflop: Don't I look pretty, too?

 King Crusty: Of course, Dandyfop, you look um...

 Queen Clementine: You look lovely, dear, but where are PJ and Tiara? They're late!

Storyteller: Suddenly the two princesses burst through the door. They were covered in dirt and muddy water sprayed everywhere!

 Prince Dandyfop: Yuck! Now my jacket is filthy!

Queen Clementine: Look at the state of the two of you! What have you been doing?

 **Princess Tiara:** Splashing in mudddy puddles! We found out we both like the same things.

 King Crusty: Goodness! You look so um...

Princess PJ: Happy? We are! We're the best friends ever!

Queen Clementine: Well, it's too late to change now. Just hurry up! Supper is served and the dancing is about to begin.

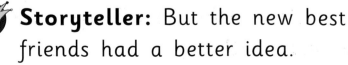 **Storyteller:** But the new best friends had a better idea.

Princess Tiara: I think dancing is boring. Let's have a food fight instead.

 Princess PJ: Great idea! Take that, Dandyfop!

 Storyteller: And do you know what? Princess PJ and Princess Tiara were absolutely right!

START READING is a series of highly enjoyable books for beginner readers. **The books have been carefully graded to match the Book Bands widely used in schools.** This enables readers to be sure they choose books that match their own reading ability.

Look out for the Band colour on the book in our Start Reading logo.

The Bands are:

Pink Band 1A & 1B

Red Band 2

Yellow Band 3

Blue Band 4

Green Band 5

Orange Band 6

Turquoise Band 7

Purple Band 8

Gold Band 9

START READING books can be read independently or shared with an adult. They promote the enjoyment of reading through satisfying stories, plays and non-fiction narratives, which are supported by fun illustrations and photographs.

Karen Wallace was brought up in a log cabin in Canada. She has written lots of different books for children and even won a few awards. Karen likes writing funny books because she can laugh at her own jokes!

Cathy Brett has been scribbling all her life — first on pieces of paper, on walls and sometimes on her sister! She later became a fashion designer and an author/illustrator. Her scribbles have appeared in lots of books, in shop windows and even on beach towels. Cathy likes listening to really loud rock music!